I0746541
Spartan + FRIENDS

Hazel and Spartan Spread Cheer
Colouring and Literacy Book
Consolidating phonics knowledge with extended decodable text.

Word Count
Approx. 305 words

Focus Phonics Sounds
or → horse, forward, morning
oo → gloom, bloom
ch → cheer, children, reached, each
sh → she, brushed, shining, share
th → through, them, that, there, with
wh → when, whisper, while

High-Frequency Words
and, the, of, in, on, with, to, for, is, it, they, he, she, we,
was, said, all, your, you, I, that, this, here, there, by, from, at,
his, her, had, some, were, one, as, so, out, then, not, their, when

Irregular Words
was, were, you, your, they, their, are, one, some, come, here, there, again

Practice Words
hospital, nursing, home, garden, roses, grandpas, grandmas, kindness,
cheer, children, nurse, wheelchair, garden, patient, visit, cuddle, gentle,
hearts, brave, caring, joyful, sparkle

Teacher Prep Before Reading
Review ai and ee diagraphs with word cards. (day, beamed, feel)
Practice igh trigraphs. (light, night, kind)
Practice oo vowel sound. (bloom, gloom, hooves)
Practice high frequency words, for quick recognition.
Introduce the key story words

Hazel groomed Spartan, his coat shining black,
she brushed out his mane, smoothed the hair
on his back.
Miss Laura said, "Let's go do something kind,
let's spread some cheer and warm some hearts."

"We'll ride to the home, where elders reside.
They'll love to see Spartan, and feel some horse-pride."
Hazel beamed brightly, she patted Spartan's mane,
"Let's bring folks a smile and joy to their day."

They rode to the parklands, near roses in bloom,
where grandmas and grandpas sat out in the gloom.
"Clip-clop, clip-clop," Spartan walked with care,
the old friends leaned forward, glad they were there.

One man said softly, "I once rode a bay, a strong little cob that could trot all day."

A lady reached out, with a tear in her eye,
"He feels just like mine did, all those years drifting by."
Hazel felt proud as Spartan stood still,
she let them all pat him, with patience and skill.

Then Miss Laura smiled, "One more stop today,
the children's ward garden is not far away."
Through winding streets, they clip-clopped along,
Hazel hummed gently a soft, happy song.

At the hospital gate, the nurses came fast,
"The children are ready, you're here at last!"
In the small garden, the children came near,
some hugged Spartan's nose, others
grinned ear to ear.

One boy in a wheelchair let out a loud cheer.
"I've dreamed of a horse,
and now there is one here!"

Hazel said kindly, "He's gentle, not wild.
He loves to be patted by every child."

When the visit was done, Hazel whispered that night,
"Spartan brings joy and makes hearts feel light."

Activities (for after reading)

1. Re-read the story and circle words with the ar sound. (Garden)

2. Find and <u>underline</u> all the words with or sound. (forward)

3. Write 3 new sentences with ch sounds. (children)

____

____

____

____

____

____

____

4. What was your favourite part of the story?_______________

5. Fill the gap: "Let's go do something _____________.

Activities (for after reading)

6. Write a short story about what one of the elderly people at the nursing home might have been remembering when they saw Spartan.

____

____

____

____

____

____

____

____

____

Activities (for after reading)

7. Write some words that rhyme with cheer.

____

____

8. Can you name the places Hazel and Miss Laura went?

____

____

____

9. Why do you think Miss Laura wanted Hazel and Spartan to visit the nursing home and hospital?

____

____

____

____

Activities (for after reading)

10. Can you retell the important parts of the story?

____

____

11. What was your favourite part of story?

____

____

____

12. Draw a map showing Hazel and Spartan's journey to "Spread Cheer." Start at the stables and show all the places they visit along the way.

Activities (for after reading)

13. Find all the rhyming words in the story and write them below.
For example kind – find – mind
Then add your own to rhyme with those words.

____

____

____

____

14. Complete the words with the missing sounds:

g___den

ch___r

fl___ers

str___ts

bl___m

15. Colour in all of the story pages.

How to draw
Spartan

Spartan + FRIENDS

www.ingramcontent.com/pod-product-compliance
Lightning Source LLC
Chambersburg PA
CBHW040548170726
48295CB00012B/633